This Book Belongs To:

AFRAID OF MONSTERS NO MORE

By Vanessa
Santiago-Jerman

Hello Parents

First I want to thank you for purchasing Afraid of Monsters No More. I hope that it helps in getting your little ones to be more at ease with transitioning from your bed to their own, as well as learning that there are no such thing as Monsters.

If you are reading this book to your child please be very descriptive in voice and change up the tone and voice with each character. This helps keep children interested. Try to get an involved with them understanding the lesson in the story by asking questions after the story is over.

For example: Why do you think Arron is afraid to sleep alone? Why do you think Arron's mom took him to the pet store? What are some things Arron could have done so he wouldn't be afraid to sleep alone?

I hope this book is helpful and I would like you to become a fan of Brand New Happy Moon Be sure to join our mailing list at:
www.brandnewhappymoonpublishing.com

Dedicated to the children of our future,
Author Vanessa~

"Arron sweetie, it's time to get out of the tub," said mommy.

"Please, just five more minutes mommy," Arron responded.

"Well ok, but no more than five minutes. The water will get cold and we don't need you sick."

Arron smiled as he finished playing with his cars in the tub.

Five minutes later, mom unplugged the water and said, "OK young man, we have to get you ready for bed."

"But, mom!" Arron chimed in, "I am afraid."

"Afraid of what?" asked mom.

"Monsters! There are monsters in my room," Arron answered.

"Honey, there are no such thing as monsters. They are not real."

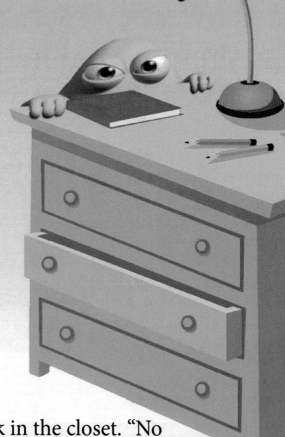

Mom takes Arron to his room and they look in the closet. "No monsters here," said mom.

They look behind the door. "No monsters here," said Mom.

They look under Arron's bed. "No monsters here," said Mom.

They looked by the side of the dresser. "No monsters here," said Mom.

"Now that we made sure there are no monsters, I'll plug in your night light. You can go to sleep now and not be afraid."

Arron replied, "OK, Mommy."

Like clockwork, at around 11:00 pm Arron came running into his parent's room and jumps in their bed.

"Mommy, daddy there are monsters in my room. Can I sleep with you?" Arron said. Mom looked at daddy and said, "…just one more night. I have an idea." That night Arron slept with his parents again.

The next morning after breakfast, mommy told Arron they were going out to get a surprise gift.

Arron was beyond excited when they arrived outside of the local pet store.

"Mommy, mommy, are we getting a pet?", said a very excited Arron.

"Well, I was thinking you could pick out a pet to keep you safe at night, would you like that sweetie?"

"Yes, mommy! Yes!"

Arron and mom take a walk through the pet store to find the perfect pet.

As they walk by the turtles, Arron said, "I want a turtle, but it would be too slow and the monsters will get me." So, he keeps looking.

He passes the fish tanks and baby sharks. "I would get a shark, but he would make such a mess with all the water from his tank." So, he keeps looking.

He passes the snakes. "Eew! I don't like snakes mommy. They scare me as much as monsters." So, he keeps looking.

"A kitten, how cute!" says Arron, "but he couldn't hurt a fly." So, he keeps looking.

As he approaches the puppies, he says, "I think I found the perfect pet."
"I would like a puppy." He took a few walks around the puppy cages and said this is the one. He wasn't too big, and wasn't too little. He was a beagle and he was the cutest thing you ever did see, with his big floppy ears. Mommy had the attendant get the puppy who already had all his shots. Then, they paid for Arron's new best friend.

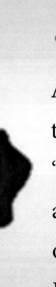

That night before bed, Arron took his bath and slipped into his PJ's. Mom tucked him in as usual and said, "Ok good night, Arron," as she placed Blake beside him. "You two have a good night sleep," and she kissed him on the forehead, turned on his night light and went to bed.

That night, Arron felt confident. He was not afraid to go to bed because he had his new best friend with him, his puppy Blake.

Just when he was about to doze off, he saw a shadow on the wall.

Oh no, not again he thought.

Arron screamed, "Daddy, Daddy!" as he ran into his parents room.

Blake was not far behind him.

"What is it?" his dad asked as he jumped out of bed.

"There is a monster in my room!"

Dad slipped on his slippers, gently took Arron by the hand and said, "Son, there are no such thing as monsters. Come on and we will see what all the fuss is about." Arron grabbed tight onto Dad's hand as he led him tippy-toed to his room.

He crept closer and closer to his room. Arron peeked inside still holding on to daddy's hand.

"There it is," he pointed. Dad took a peak inside and chuckled. "That's not a monster, son."

Arron said, "Yes, it is daddy. Look it's moving."

" Son, that is no monster. It is just a shadow of the tree outside of your window."

Arron responded, "…a shadow? What's that?"

"The moonlight is shining on the tree outside. This causes it to create a shadow through your window and onto your wall, kind of like a reflection of the tree." Dad said.

Dad said, "See look at this," as he closed Arron's blinds and curtains. The shadow disappeared.

He then opened it back up, so Arron could see that what he was saying was true.

Arron said, "So, there are no monsters?"

Dad said ."No, son. There are no such thing as monsters."

Arron was so relieved, he gave his daddy a big hug.

He grabbed Blake and snuggled back in bed. This was the first night in 4 years that Arron slept in bed alone. He is now afraid of monsters no more.

THE END.

I, _____

(your name)

have read this book

☐ once

☐ twice

☐ again and again

BRAND NEW HAPPY MOON PUBLISHING
ANTHOLOGY CONTRIBUTOR

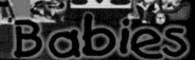

COMING SOON!
A BEDTIME BABIES BEDSIDE READ!

Babies

Brand New Happy Moon
Noemi Waits For Tomorrow
Written by: PB&J

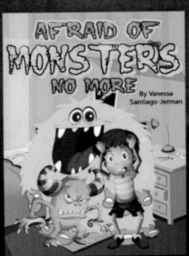

AFRAID OF MONSTERS NO MORE
By Vanessa Santiago-Jerman

BRAND NEW HAPPY MOON PUBLISHING
Goodnight Magic Shoes
Author Felicia Capers

Let Reading Pay Off

Win Reward Points to buy
cool games, clothing, books,
art supplies and more...

Bringing Readers Worlds Beyond Their Imagination

Reading Chart

Book Title	End Date	Begin Date	Completed?	RATE ME!
			Y N	
			Y N	
			Y N	
			Y N	
			Y N	
			Y N	
			Y N	
			Y N	
			Y N	
			Y N	

See How...

Join our website
www.brandnewhappymoonpublishing.com

You Can Start
With These

Brand New Happy Moon Publishing

Noemi
Waits
For Tomorrow

Written by: PB&J

BRAND NEW HAPPY MOON PUBLISHING

Afraid of
Monsters
No More

1.

2.

BRAND NEW HAPPY MOON PUBLISHING

Goodnight
Magic
Shoes
Author Felicia Capers

WOW!

LOOK AT ALL OUR FRIENDS!

AND WE HAVE SO MANY MORE. COMING TO STAY WITH US IN 2017

www.brandnewhappymoonpublishing.com

Made in the USA
Middletown, DE
20 October 2022

13040863R00027